The Dream Date
Debate

TWO of a kind ™

The Dream Date Debate

by Megan Stine

from the series created by
Robert Griffard
& Howard Adler

■ HarperEntertainment
An Imprint of **HarperCollins***Publishers*

A PARACHUTE PRESS BOOK

A PARACHUTE PRESS BOOK

Parachute Publishing, L.L.C.
156 Fifth Avenue
Suite 302
New York, NY 10010

Published by
HarperEntertainment
An Imprint of HarperCollins*Publishers*
10 East 53rd Street, New York, NY 10022-5299

TWO OF A KIND books created and produced by Parachute Press, L.L.C., in cooperation with Dualstar Publications, a division of Dualstar Entertainment Group, LLC, published by HarperEntertainment, an imprint of HarperCollins Publishers.

ISBN 0-06-009324-2

HarperCollins®, ®, and HarperEntertainment™ are trademarks of HarperCollins Publishers Inc.

First printing: April 2003

Printed in the United States of America

Visit HarperEntertainment on the World Wide Web at
www.harpercollins.com

10 9 8 7 6 5 4 3 2 1

CHAPTER ONE

"So who's up for the Dream Date Debate?" Ashley Burke asked, looking around at her friends.

It was Saturday afternoon and they were all hanging out in the Student Union at the White Oak Academy for Girls. White Oak was the boarding school where Ashley and her twin sister, Mary-Kate, were enrolled.

"I'm in," Elise Van Hook cheered.

"Me, too!" Summer Sorenson added eagerly.

"It sounds like a nineteen fifties board game," Ashley's roommate, Phoebe Cahill, said, shaking her head.

"Well, it's not," Ashley said. "It's going to be the most exciting event in White Oak history!"

"At least Mrs. Pritchard is going to let us First Formers play this year," Samantha Kramer said. First Form was what they called the seventh grade at White Oak.

"Yeah, why should the upperclassmen have all the fun?" Elise added.

The Dream Date Debate was a game the older students at White Oak and the Harrington School for Boys played every spring. It was like a TV game show, except it was held in the Harrington auditorium. Couples paired up to answer questions about each other. Whichever team got the most answers right won either a romantic dream date or an awesome pizza party with their friends.

"I just wish the guys would get here so we can start practicing," Samantha complained.

So do I, Ashley thought, twisting a long strand of her wavy blond hair around one finger. She couldn't help imagining the awesome date she and her boyfriend, Ross, would have if they won the game.

"Can't you just picture it?" she said dreamily. "Ross and I riding under the stars in a horse-drawn carriage. To a fancy restaurant for a candlelit dinner! It will be so totally romantic!"

"Whoa, hold on," Phoebe said. "You haven't won yet!"

"That's true," Ashley agreed quickly. "And there'll be tons of competition. But wouldn't it be cool if we *did* win?"

"So what's the point of this whole debate thing again?" Summer asked.

Summer was one of Ashley's friends. She was beautiful and blond and funny. But sometimes she could be a little bit ditzy.

"It's supposed to settle the question, Who is the coolest couple? You know, who knows the most about each other and stuff," Ashley explained.

"That's not fair. You and Ross know practically everything about each other," Samantha said.

"Well, that *is* true," Ashley admitted. "Sorry, girls, but we're probably going to win that dream date."

"Why should the rest of us even bother playing?" Phoebe teased her.

"Hey, I'm not giving up so easily!" Samantha protested. "Nathan and I want that pizza party. If we practice enough, I think we have a good chance of winning. Even against Ashley and Ross!"

"Nathan Berger?" Elise wrinkled her nose. "But he's not your boyfriend. He's just a friend."

"Exactly," Samantha said, nodding. "That's why we'll make a great team. We already know a lot about each other." She held up a sheet of paper.

"And we're going to memorize every one of these practice questions—if the guys ever get here!"

Ashley glanced at the clock on the wall. *I wish they'd hurry,* she thought. Not just because she wanted to see Ross and practice for the Dream Date Debate. But she also had a huge homework project to work on later for history class.

The door to the Student U opened. Ross and several other guys from Harrington walked into the lounge area, followed by Mary-Kate.

"Hi!" Ashley called to her sister. Then she hurried over to Ross. "Hey," she said, giving him a big hug.

Quickly, she headed toward the two new bean-bag chairs in the corner. She knew that was Ross's favorite spot.

There isn't anything I don't know about him! she told herself.

"Hang on, I want to get a soda," Ross called.

Ashley watched as he walked to the drink machine and bought two cans of soda. Cola for himself, ginger ale for her. It was her new favorite drink these days.

And he knows everything about me, too, she thought. *How can we not win the game?*

The Student U was getting crowded now. Ashley could definitely feel the buzz in the air. Everyone

4

was psyched about the Dream Date Debate.

"Do you want to team up with me?" Ashley heard Dylan Tunnell ask Summer.

"Maybe," Summer said. "Let's practice a little and see how we do."

Hmmm, Ashley thought. They'd make a good couple. She glanced around. Mary-Kate and Jordan Marshall made a good couple, too.

Ashley watched them talking and laughing on the far side of the room. Her sister and Jordan had been going out for only a short while, but they really seemed to like each other.

They look so cute together, Ashley thought. Jordan's sandy-blond hair was almost the exact same color as Mary-Kate's.

"So what do we have to do?" Ross asked when they were both snuggled into the beanbag chairs.

Ashley took a page out of her binder. "I have a list of questions the older girls were given last year. We can use them to practice."

"Okay, but tell me again how this thing works," Ross said.

Ashley nodded and gave him the details. The girls from each team would go backstage first so they couldn't hear what the guys were saying. Then the game host would ask the guys questions about their partners. The guys had to give the right answers. Then they would switch and the girls would answer questions about the guys.

"And we'll get one point for every question we get right," Ashley explained.

"Okay, shoot," Ross said after he took a swig of his soda.

Ashley looked down at the list and read the first question. "What's your favorite color?" she asked.

As if I don't know that one, she thought. Blue. He wore a blue shirt almost every day. It looked so great with his dark hair and blue eyes.

"Red," Ross said matter-of-factly.

"Red?" Ashley said. "That can't be right."

"Are you going to tell me what my favorite color is?" Ross asked.

Behind her, Ashley heard someone snicker. She looked over and saw Dana Woletsky sitting in one of the overstuffed armchairs. Dana was the one girl at White Oak who didn't seem to like Ashley very much. Ashley felt the same way about Dana.

"Ashley doesn't even know what Ross's favorite color is," Dana announced loudly to the whole room. She laughed as if she had just told the funniest joke in the world.

"I do, too!" Ashley said.

A few of Ashley's friends looked up and giggled.

"Don't worry, Ashley," Samantha teased her. "I'll invite you to the pizza party when I win."

Ashley felt herself blush. How embarrassing! *Oh, well. I'll get the rest of them right,* she thought.

She looked at the list again. "Okay, Ross. If you had to eat the same thing every day for a week, would you rather have pizza or candy?"

Easy, she told herself with a smile. Candy. Ross was a gummy-bear freak.

"Pizza," Ross answered.

"Huh? But you *love* candy!" Ashley argued.

"Well, yeah, but I wouldn't want to eat it every single day for a week," Ross said. "I'd get totally sick of it."

Ashley sighed. "Fine. But try to get this one right," she said.

"*You're* the one who's getting them wrong," Ross reminded her.

"Okay, okay," Ashley said. "Let's see. What's your favorite sport?" *Now, that's a* really *easy one,* she thought. Baseball. Ross was one of the stars on the Harrington team.

"Football," Ross said.

"No way!" Ashley cried. "You don't even *play* football!"

7

"I thought you meant my favorite sport to watch on TV," Ross said.

Ashley threw up her hands. This definitely wasn't turning out the way she thought it would. Not at all!

"Maybe we should stop practicing for a while," she said. "Why don't you help me come up with an idea for my history report instead?"

"You really need a good grade on that, huh?" Ross said.

"Definitely," Ashley said. "An A would pull up my grade for this term. Got any ideas?"

Ross shrugged. "Um, not really," he said. "History isn't my favorite subject."

Mary-Kate tapped Ashley on the shoulder. Jordan was with her. "How's it going?" Mary-Kate asked.

"We're taking a little break," Ashley replied. "How about you? Are you guys practicing hard?"

Mary-Kate smiled at Jordan. "Oh, we're not practicing," she said. "We're going to play a video game."

Ashley blinked. "How come?"

"We don't need to practice," Jordan said. "We're totally in the zone. When we were going over those questions from last year . . ."

". . . we started finishing each other's sentences," Mary-Kate said.

"All right!" Jordan slapped palms with Mary-Kate. "We did it again!" They both laughed.

Wow, Ashley thought. *They* are *good together!*

She glanced around the room again. Everyone was busy practicing. They all seemed like they were having so much fun. And lots of couples were getting all their practice questions right!

Maybe I shouldn't have bragged that Ross and I were going to win, she thought. *Because at this rate, we're not going to win, we're going to come in dead last!*

CHAPTER TWO

"So what's your favorite video game?" Mary-Kate asked Jordan as they walked into the back room of the Student U.

"Kung Fu Cooks totally rocks," Jordan said.

"Oh, I love that one!" Mary-Kate agreed. "With those crazy chefs trying to capture the golden egg roll?"

Jordan nodded. "We should get it for the Student U," he said.

"Definitely," Mary-Kate agreed.

Jordan is so cool, Mary-Kate thought. He liked all the same things she liked. Funny video games instead of the violent ones. Peanut butter and apple sandwiches instead of peanut butter and jelly. And

10

rock and alternative bands more than techno music.

How did I get so lucky? Mary-Kate wondered. Not only did they get along great, but Jordan was totally cute. *And the cuter he looks, the more nervous I get,* she added to herself.

She still felt a little nervous with Jordan some-times—even though they had so much in common.

"Hey, what's your favorite rock band?" Jordan asked.

"So So So," Mary-Kate answered immediately.

"Mine, too," Jordan said. "There's a concert in town next month. You want to go?"

"Totally!" Mary-Kate said.

"The tickets go on sale tonight at eight," Jordan said.

"Oh." Mary-Kate's heart sank. "Getting tickets to concerts is almost impossible at White Oak," she said. "I mean, there's only one phone in each dorm. Girls are always standing in line for it. The chances of getting through at eight o'clock are pretty slim."

"Yeah, I know," Jordan replied. "It's the same at Harrington. But I've got a better idea. Let's take the bus into town and stand in line at the ticket outlet."

"Really? Cool!" Mary-Kate jumped at the idea. "I just have to run back to my dorm to get a warmer jacket. In case it turns cold again."

"Okay," Jordan said. "I'll meet you at the bus stop."

"See you there!" Mary-Kate hurried out the door.

Now that the sun was going down, the April air was crisp. But at least it wasn't freezing the way it had been a few weeks before.

She made it across campus to Porter House in record time. A bunch of girls were hanging out in the hall, sitting on the floor.

Oh, right, Mary-Kate thought. She'd almost forgotten.

Kristen Lindquist was having a slumber party in the dorm that night. She had invited Dana, her best friend from Phipps House, and about six other girls. They were all going to sleep over in the Porter House lounge.

Dana sat on the floor, putting on nail polish. She wouldn't move her legs to let Mary-Kate get through the crammed hallway. Mary-Kate had to climb over her.

"Hey, Mary-Kate, get your sleeping bag and hang out with us!" Brooke Miller said. "We're going to play Truth or Dare."

"Sorry," Mary-Kate said. "Maybe later. I'm going into town with Jordan right now."

"Jordan?" Brooke asked. "You guys are entering

the Dream Date Debate together, aren't you?"

Mary-Kate nodded. "Yup."

"Well, good luck," Brooke went on. "Maybe you'll win."

"I doubt it," Dana said.

"Excuse me?" Mary-Kate stared at Dana.

"Face it," Dana said. "You're not going to win. Nobody's going to beat me and Nicholas."

"Nicholas?" Mary-Kate said, surprised. Nicholas Sampson was a snobby rich kid who usually hung out in the computer lab. He didn't really seem like Dana's type.

"Since when are you two going out?" Mary-Kate asked.

Dana shrugged. "We're not. But we're a perfect team for the Dream Date." She blew on her nails. "Keep practicing, though, Mary-Kate. Maybe you and Jordan will get second prize." She paused. "Oh, wait. There *is* no second prize. Sorry."

I don't believe her! Mary-Kate thought. The only prize Dana Woletsky could ever win was the grand trophy for the most annoying person ever.

Mary-Kate tried her hardest to ignore Dana. She hurried up to her room to get her jacket and scarf. Then she ran all the way back across campus again to meet Jordan at the bus stop.

"Hi," he said, smiling at her.

"Hi," Mary-Kate said breathlessly. She gave him a happy-to-see-you-too smile. But inside she was still fuming about Dana.

"What's wrong?" he asked.

"Oh, nothing," Mary-Kate said. "It's just Dana. She thinks she and Nicholas are going to win the Dream Date Debate."

Jordan grinned. "She'll have to beat us first," he said.

"It *would* be cool if we won, wouldn't it?" Mary-Kate said.

Jordan nodded. "We'd take the pizza party prize, right?"

"Definitely," Mary-Kate agreed.

"We'd order mushrooms," he said, looking into her eyes. "And . . . "

"Pepperoni?" Mary-Kate finished.

"Perfect!" Jordan said, giving her a high five.

But when their hands touched, he closed his fingers around hers. Then he swung their arms down so he was holding Mary-Kate's hand. And he didn't let go until the bus came and they had to climb up the steps one at a time.

This is amazing! Mary-Kate thought. Her hand felt all tingly now, but she was a little nervous, too.

She glanced at Jordan. Would he try to kiss her tonight? She wouldn't mind that one bit!

When they got off the bus, it was almost six o'clock. The ticket outlet was at the end of a cute little street of shops and restaurants. About forty people were already standing in line, waiting for the tickets to go on sale.

Mary-Kate and Jordan joined the line, and Jordan took her hand again. The two of them talked and talked as they waited for the ticket outlet to open.

Finally it did, at eight o'clock sharp. Very slowly, the line began to move.

"I hope this doesn't take too long," Mary-Kate said, starting to worry a little. She had to be back in her dorm by nine o'clock—before the front door was locked. "We've got to get the eight-thirty shuttle back to campus."

"Or what? You'll turn into a pumpkin?" Jordan teased.

"Worse," Mary-Kate told him. "I'll be locked out of the dorm!"

"Don't worry." Jordan checked his watch. "It's only eight-fifteen. We'll make it back before nine."

"I hope so," Mary-Kate said, sighing.

The line was moving really, really slowly. But so

far this date had been perfect. The moon was shining brightly above them now. And Jordan was still holding her hand.

Suddenly, a gentle breeze began to blow. A leaf from a nearby oak tree swirled and flew into Mary-Kate's hair.

Mary-Kate reached up to get the leaf. Jordan reached for it at the same time.

"I think it's stuck," he said, leaning toward her a little more.

He brushed the leaf away and smiled at her. His face was very close to hers, but he didn't move away.

Mary-Kate got a fluttering feeling in her stomach. Was Jordan going to kiss her?

Jordan bent his head and leaned in even closer.

He is *going to kiss me!* Mary-Kate realized. Her heart pounded in her chest as she closed her eyes.

"Hey—move up, you guys!" someone behind them said.

Startled, Mary-Kate and Jordan jumped away from each other. She glanced at the line in front of them. It had finally moved. A lot. Only one person stood in front of them at the ticket window.

"Come on, move up," another guy behind them said impatiently. "You're next."

Jordan quickly dropped Mary-Kate's hand.

A little disappointed, Mary-Kate followed him as they moved up close behind the girl in front of them. She was a teenager with long red braids, and she was arguing with the guy in the ticket window. "Don't you have anything better than the twentieth row?" she begged. "I have to sit up front!"

The ticket seller shrugged. "Sorry. How about the balcony?"

"No way." The girl shook her head.

"She sure is picky," Mary-Kate whispered to Jordan as the girl and the ticket seller began to argue again. "She's taking forever."

"You're lucky to even get these seats," the ticket seller told the girl. "Take them or lose them."

Finally the girl bought her tickets and left, grumbling.

"Don't worry," Jordan said to Mary-Kate. "We'll make the bus. It's only a couple of blocks away."

He stepped forward and pushed his money through the ticket window.

"Two for So So So," he said really fast. "Just give us the best you've got. We're kind of in a rush."

"Okay," the ticket guy said. "You're in the twenty-third row. Here you go. All sales are final, by the way."

"Fine." Jordan grabbed the tickets and turned away.

Mary-Kate checked her watch and gasped. "It's eight-twenty-seven. Let's go!"

She and Jordan ran as fast as they could, all the way down the street. They took a left, then sprinted another block toward the bus stop. The bus wasn't there.

Mary-Kate checked her watch again. Eight-thirty-two. "Oh, no! We missed it!" she cried.

"Guess we'll have to wait for the nine o'clock bus," Jordan mumbled. "Sorry, Mary-Kate. I really thought we'd make it."

"It's okay," she told him—even though she knew she'd be in major trouble when she got back to Porter House.

"So what are you going to do?" Jordan asked. "I mean, do they really lock your dorm right at nine? Harrington's curfew isn't until ten."

Mary-Kate tried to ignore the sinking feeling in her stomach. "Remember what I said about turning into a pumpkin?" she asked Jordan.

He nodded.

Mary-Kate sighed. "Make that pumpkin pie."

CHAPTER THREE

"Be careful or they'll see us," Mary-Kate warned Jordan when they reached Porter House at nine-thirty.

From the front walkway she could see lights blazing in the first-floor lounge. Kristen's slumber party was in full swing.

"We can hide here," Jordan said. He stepped behind a tree.

Mary-Kate joined him. She was glad that Jordan was with her. He had walked her to her dorm when they got off the bus, just to make sure she was safe.

"Can't you tap on the window and get one of those girls to let you in?" Jordan asked.

"No way," Mary-Kate whispered. "Dana's in

19

there. She'd rat on me to Miss Viola for sure."

Miss Viola was the dorm mother who lived in Porter House.

"I think I have to climb in a window," Mary-Kate decided finally. "And hope no one sees me."

"Ouch," Jordan said, shaking his head. "I had no idea they were so strict at White Oak."

"So you won't get in trouble at all?" Mary-Kate asked. "What if you get back later than ten? The last shuttle bus is at nine-forty-five."

"No problem," Jordan said. "Mr. Bromley never locks the front door on time."

That's cool, Mary-Kate thought. She wished Miss Viola would be so laid-back!

Mary-Kate checked out the windows near the front hallway. The one on the left looked easy to open. "I'm going in there," she whispered to Jordan.

He nodded. "I'll wait till you're in. Good luck."

"Thanks. I had fun tonight. See you soon," she said softly.

Jordan nodded. "Me, too," he said. "Bye."

Mary-Kate slipped out from behind the tree and hurried toward the dorm. She peered through the window.

She carefully lifted the window. It slid open without making too much noise.

Probably no one would hear anything anyway, Mary-Kate told herself. *Everyone's talking in the lounge.*

Luckily, the window ledge was low, so she didn't have to boost herself up. She climbed in, closed the window quickly, and hurried up the front stairs before anyone could see her.

Phew! Mary-Kate thought. *That was close. I am so lucky I didn't get caught.*

But on the bright side, she and Jordan had seats for the So So So concert. And Jordan had *almost* kissed her. What a night!

"Mary-Kate, wake up!" Her roommate, Campbell Smith, shook her awake the next morning. "Mrs. Pritchard wants everyone downstairs—pronto!"

Mary-Kate sat up in bed and glanced at her clock. It was still pretty early on Sunday morning. And Mrs. Pritchard almost *never* came to visit the dorms.

"What's going on?" Mary-Kate asked, yawning.

"Don't know," Campbell said. "But The Head looks really mad."

The Head was their nickname for Mrs. Pritchard. She was the headmistress at White Oak.

"Someone's in big trouble," Campbell added.

Trouble? Mary-Kate froze. *Uh-oh,* she thought.

Maybe someone saw me climbing in the window last night.

But that wasn't possible. She had slipped up the stairs and through the hall without running into a single person. Even Campbell hadn't missed her. When she'd gotten back to their dorm room, her roommate hadn't seemed surprised.

She probably figured I was hanging out somewhere else in the dorm, Mary-Kate thought. *Like at Kristen's slumber party.*

Mary-Kate grabbed her robe and followed Campbell out into the hallway. "What kind of trouble?" she asked.

Campbell shrugged. "I didn't get any details."

Most of the girls from Porter House were already gathered at the bottom of the stairs.

Kristin and her friends from the slumber party were huddled near the door to the lounge. Ashley was sitting on a bench against the wall.

Mrs. Pritchard stood stiffly, waiting for the latecomers to arrive. Miss Viola was by her side.

"I am sorry to say that we have a serious problem in this dorm," Mrs. Pritchard announced. "Someone apparently sneaked into Porter House last night after hours—and that person left a window open in the foyer."

"I found a muddy footprint under the window," Miss Viola added. "The footprint wasn't there when I locked the door."

Mary-Kate's heart started beating twice as fast. *I'm sure I closed that window!* she thought. *I couldn't have left it open—could I?*

Mrs. Pritchard pointed to the window. "Unfortunately, a raccoon got in." The headmistress paused and looked around the room. "As you may imagine, wild animals can do a good deal of damage in a house," she went on. "This one got into Miss Viola's kitchen and made a huge mess."

"Uh-oh," Mary-Kate heard Ashley mumble.

"Miss Viola called me early this morning. There's food and garbage all over the kitchen floor," Mrs. Pritchard said. "And the raccoon also scratched up the new paint on the cabinets."

Oh, no! Mary-Kate thought. *This is getting worse and worse!*

Mrs. Pritchard crossed her arms and stared at the girls. "Well, I shouldn't have to say anything more. But I expect the responsible person to come forward. There's a lot of cleaning up to do—to say nothing about the fact that we have rules in White Oak dorms."

Mary-Kate bit a fingernail and tried to think

back. She couldn't be *positive* that she closed the window. Or maybe she closed it—but not all the way.

What if I left it open a little? she wondered. *Could a raccoon possibly have squeezed in?*

Mrs. Pritchard stood there waiting for someone to speak up. No one stirred. Mary-Kate could feel how nervous everyone was.

Mrs. Pritchard shook her head. "Well, I'm sorry to say this," she said, "but until the guilty person speaks up, Porter House will not be participating in the Dream Date Debate."

Several girls gasped. Mary-Kate glanced at her sister. Ashley looked totally disappointed.

It's not fair! Mary-Kate thought. *Mrs. Pritchard is punishing everyone for something only one person did.*

"I sincerely hope that someone will come forward soon," Mrs. Pritchard said. Then she and Miss Viola disappeared into Miss Viola's apartment.

As soon as they were gone, the foyer began to buzz.

"Who do you think did it?" Campbell whispered to Mary-Kate.

Mary-Kate just shrugged. She couldn't tell her that *she* might have done it.

"Did you see anyone sneaking in last night?" Dana asked Kristen loudly.

"No," Kristen said, shaking her head. "But it must be someone who was out last night. *You* went out last night, didn't you, Mary-Kate?"

Mary-Kate didn't answer, and Kristen laughed.

"Well, one thing's for sure. Whoever did it is going to be in hot water," Phoebe said.

"What are we going to do?" Ashley said to her sister. "Mrs. Pritchard *can't* cancel the Dream Date. It was going to be so much fun!"

"I know," Mary-Kate agreed. Her head was spinning now. She didn't know *what* to do. Should she admit that she was the person who had sneaked in last night?

And then what would happen?

Slowly, the girls began to head back to their rooms.

"It's just not fair," Ashley complained, joining Mary-Kate on the stairs.

"I know," Campbell said. "The guilty person should just 'fess up and face the punishment. No matter how awful it is. Right, Mary-Kate?"

"Yeah," Mary-Kate said glumly.

Except the guilty person is probably me!

CHAPTER FOUR

"I guess maybe I'm glad Dream Date is canceled," Ashley said to Phoebe the next morning. The two of them were walking to history class.

"Glad? *You*?" Phoebe said. "Get real. You're totally bummed."

"I know, I know," Ashley admitted. "But I *should* be glad."

Phoebe sighed and ran her fingers through her curly dark hair. "Okay, I give up. How come?"

"Because now I'll have more time to work on my history report," Ashley explained.

"Oh, right. The Paul Revere thing." Phoebe nodded. Everyone in class had to do a report on Paul Revere, but they had to pick which aspect of his life they wanted to write about. It was due in a week, next Monday.

"I'm doing an illustrated manuscript with old-fashioned calligraphy," Phoebe said. "What's your idea?"

"Well, I have to talk to Mr. Montgomery about it," Ashley said. "But I'm hoping to do something on the fashions of the times."

Phoebe laughed. "The *fashions* of Paul Revere?"

"Hey—fashion is important," Ashley argued.

"*Totally*. Don't worry, I'm on your side!" Phoebe said. "By the way, how do you like my new jeans?"

"New?" Ashley did a double take and stared at Phoebe's outfit. Her roommate loved vintage clothes. She never wore *anything* that wasn't at least ten years old. "Wow. Those *are* new, aren't they? How come?"

"It's so retro to wear brand-new jeans," Phoebe explained. "I mean, everyone goes for jeans that are sand-washed or tea-stained or whatever, right? But in the fifties you weren't cool unless your jeans were brand new. So I figure this is a vintage look!"

"Oh, I get it." Ashley laughed. "Very clever." Just then, out of the corner of her eye, she spotted her history teacher. "There's Mr. Montgomery. I'll talk to you later, Phoebe."

Ashley hurried to catch her teacher before class started. Quickly, she explained her plan for doing a report on what Paul Revere would have worn.

Mr. Montgomery raised his eyebrows. "I don't know, Ashley," he said. "That's an interesting idea. But I think it would be better if you'd stick to something with more historical importance."

"But this *has* historical importance," Ashley argued. "I saw a program on public TV once. It was about how the clothes people wore totally affected the way they lived and worked."

"Well," Mr. Montgomery said, thinking. "Okay. I'll let you do it on one condition."

"What?" Ashley asked.

"Find three pieces of clothing that remind us of Paul Revere's time," her teacher said. "Any items of clothing that are designed in a way to remind us of colonial fashions. I'll leave it up to you to figure out the rest. All right?"

Ashley nodded. "I can do that," she said. It shouldn't be that hard. Fashion was definitely her specialty!

The bell was about to ring as Ashley spotted Ross standing out in the hall. She hurried over to him.

"I have to go shopping after school," she said, "for my history project. Want to come?"

"Shopping for history?" Ross teased. "What's

next—accessories for algebra? Lip gloss for Latin?"

"Why does everyone treat me like I'm a fashion diva?" Ashley complained as she adjusted the knot on her totally fabulous cashmere scarf.

"Because you love it when we do?" Ross asked.

"Yeah, I guess that's true," Ashley admitted with a smile. "Can you meet me at the bus stop at three?" Ross nodded and Ashley raced into class.

On the way into town that afternoon, she told him about her project.

"Whoa," Ross said. "Three things that might have been worn when Paul Revere was alive. That sounds hard. Where are you going to find old stuff like that?"

"Easy," Ashley said as they got off the bus. "I'll show you."

Ashley led the way to a thrift shop at the end of a narrow one-way street. Inside, used clothes hung on long racks up and down the store.

"This is Phoebe's favorite place," Ashley explained. "Now all we have to do is find something that looks like it came from the seventeen seventies."

Ross walked down one aisle and yanked a pair of burgundy velvet bell-bottom pants off the rack.

"How about these?" he asked.

"They're from the *nineteen* seventies," Ashley said.

"Are you sure?" Ross stared at the pants.

"Trust me," Ashley said. "I know vintage British mod when I see it. I've seen tons of it—in Phoebe's closet!"

Ross laughed and wandered toward the back of the store. Ashley looked through rack after rack of shirts, pants, and jackets. There wasn't a thing she could use. Nothing.

"This is going to be harder than I thought," Ashley mumbled. Suddenly she wasn't so sure that the topic of fashions of Paul Revere was such a great idea.

"Any luck?" Ross asked when they'd been in the store for half an hour.

Ashley shook her head. "I have to find three things, Ross!" she moaned. "Or I'll flunk this project! And I really need a good grade."

Ross thought for a minute. "Isn't there another thrift store down at the recycling center?" he said.

"Good idea!" Ashley perked up. "I totally forgot about that one. And we can stop in the bookstore afterward."

"Fine with me," Ross said.

"I want to find a book about colonial fashions," Ashley explained. "Maybe it will give me some ideas for my report."

The recycling center was only a few blocks away.

There was a small shop in back, where they sold used clothes.

It took Ashley a while to go through all the piles. But finally she found something.

"Ross, look!" She held up a man's white shirt with ruffles down the front.

"That's good," Ross said, nodding. "It looks really old-fashioned."

Finally! Ashley thought. *I can't believe I've been shopping all afternoon and bought only one thing!*

Ashley paid for the shirt and then led the way to the bookstore. Quickly, she found a book about the clothing of colonial times.

"Excellent," she said. "This is just what I needed. Check this stuff out, Ross. Short velvet pants that come only to the knees. Shiny boots with square toes and big silver buckles."

"Oh, no problem," Ross said. "I'll run home and check my closet."

Ashley laughed. "Be serious!" she told him. "I still need two more things for my report."

She flipped through the pages of the book.

"Hey, wait! Turn back," Ross said.

"What now?" Ashley asked. He was probably going to make another joke. But she flipped back a few pages.

"I've got one of those!" Ross said. He pointed to a picture of a big, clunky belt buckle.

"Are you kidding?" Ashley stared at him.

"Nope," Ross said. "That buckle is just like the one on a belt my mom gave me. She made me bring it to Harrington."

"I've never seen you wear it," Ashley said.

"And you never will," Ross told her. "It's still in my trunk at the dorm. In the basement."

"Ross, that's excellent!" Ashley cried, grabbing his arm. "Now I have to find only one more thing!"

"Uh, yeah," Ross said, glancing around the store.

Ashley thought he seemed a little nervous. "What's the matter?" she asked. "I can borrow it, can't I? I mean, I really need it for my report. And I promise not to lose it or anything."

"Okay, sure," Ross said. But he sounded just a tiny bit like he didn't want to lend it to her.

"What's wrong? Don't you trust me?" Ashley demanded.

"No, no, it's nothing like that," Ross said quickly. "You can borrow it."

"Excellent!" Ashley said. She gave Ross a quick kiss on the check. "Thanks to you, I am *so* going to get an A on this project!"

CHAPTER
FIVE

"Ashley, close the door—quick!" Mary-Kate whispered. She motioned her sister into her dorm room. "I've got to talk to you. In *private.*"

"What's up?" Ashley asked when they were alone.

Mary-Kate took a deep breath. "I've been dying to talk to you all day," she said. "But you ran off with Ross right after class."

"What's up?" Ashley asked, instantly concerned.

"I should have told you yesterday." Mary-Kate sighed. "But now that I've waited a whole day and a half, it's even worse!"

"What *is* it?" Ashley asked. She took her sister's hand. "Just spit it out. It's easier that way."

Right, Mary-Kate thought. She took another deep breath. "You know how someone sneaked into the dorm Saturday night? Well, guess who it was?" She pointed at herself.

"You?" Ashley's eyes opened wide. "*You* let the raccoon in? It's *your* fault that Mrs. Pritchard canceled the Dream Date Debate? Oh, Mary-Kate! You must feel awful!"

"I do!" Mary-Kate blurted out, glad that her sister understood. "Except I *didn't* leave the window open. At least, I don't think I did. I'm not sure. See? I'm totally going crazy here! That's why I haven't said anything yet. But the rest of it is true."

"Wow." Ashley squeezed Mary-Kate's hand. "What happened?"

Mary-Kate told her sister the whole story. About how she and Jordan went to get concert tickets and missed the eight-thirty bus back to school.

"So what are you going to do?" Ashley asked.

"I don't know," Mary-Kate said miserably. "I want to tell Mrs. Pritchard, but I don't want to get Jordan in trouble. He didn't get caught going back to his dorm."

"So just don't mention Jordan," Ashley said. "Leave him out of it."

"I hate to get in trouble," Mary-Kate said. "But

I'd hate it even more if everyone else gets punished because of me."

"Then coming clean is the right thing to do," Ashley said. "Get it over with soon, too. That way you can stop feeling guilty."

"Okay." Mary-Kate nodded. "I've made up my mind. I'll go see The Head right now."

"Do you want me to come with you?" Ashley offered.

"That would be great!" Mary-Kate said. "Thanks."

The two of them put on sweaters and headed across campus to Mrs. Pritchard's office. They had to wait twenty minutes while The Head was in a meeting.

I wish she'd hurry up, Mary-Kate thought. She was so nervous. Her hands were sweaty and her throat was dry. She just wanted to get the truth out and be done with the whole thing.

Finally Mrs. Pritchard came out. "Mary-Kate? You wanted to see me?"

"Um, yes," Mary-Kate said as they all walked into the office. She cleared her throat. "I wanted to tell you that I was late coming back to Porter House on Saturday night."

Mrs. Pritchard seemed surprised. "Oh. I see."

Mary-Kate glanced at Ashley. Ashley smiled to be encouraging. *Just spit it out*, Mary-Kate reminded herself.

"Well, I didn't *mean* to be late," Mary-Kate began. "I went into town on Saturday to buy tickets for a concert. But I missed the eight-thirty bus. By the time I got back, the dorm was locked."

Mrs. Pritchard nodded. "Go on," she said.

This is so hard! Mary-Kate thought. Especially since she couldn't tell exactly how mad The Head was going to be.

"So I climbed in the front window," Mary-Kate said. "It was only a few minutes after nine. And I honestly don't think I left the window open. But I guess I must have."

Mrs. Pritchard sighed slightly, but she didn't look too furious. "Well, I'm glad you came to see me," she said. "But you've still broken a very important rule. And Miss Viola's cabinets are quite a mess."

"I know," Mary-Kate said softly. "We saw them when we were helping clean up the kitchen." She felt terrible.

Mrs. Pritchard paced in her office a bit. "All right," she said. "Since you came forward and told the truth, Mary-Kate, I'm going to let Porter House

36

go ahead with the Dream Date Debate. But I'm afraid that *you* will not be allowed to participate. And I'll expect you to repaint Miss Viola's cabinets, too."

Phew! Mary-Kate thought. At least now the whole dorm wouldn't be mad at her for spoiling the contest.

And she was lucky Mrs. Pritchard wasn't going to suspend her or anything. The painting part of the punishment wasn't too bad, either.

But not being Jordan's partner for the Dream Date? *That* was a total bummer.

"Pass me that towel, Ashley," Mary-Kate said the next afternoon as she kneeled on Miss Viola's kitchen floor. "I dripped some paint."

"I'll get it," Ashley offered. She reached over and wiped up the white paint with a paper towel.

"Gosh, you're being so nice," Mary-Kate said. "You don't even have to help me at all. It's my punishment, not yours."

"But I want to," Ashley replied. "You always help me out when I get in trouble, right?"

"Thanks," Mary-Kate said.

Ashley picked up her paintbrush again. "Actually, there *is* something you could help me

37

with. I'm going crazy trying to find all that stuff for my Paul Revere report. I need one more piece of clothing. Any ideas?"

"You can have my blue Capri pants," Mary-Kate offered. "They're totally old."

"I need something that's totally two hundred years ago!" Ashley said. "Nothing in your closet comes close to being *that* out-of-date."

"Thanks," Mary-Kate said. "Did you try the thrift shops in town?"

"Yup." Ashley nodded. "Ross and I checked them out already."

"What a perfect boyfriend!" Mary-Kate said. "He even shops with you."

"Mmmm," Ashley said. "Well, we're not that perfect a couple."

"What's that supposed to mean?" Mary-Kate asked in surprise. "You still like Ross, don't you?"

"Of course," Ashley said. "I'm just not sure we'll win the Dream Date Debate anymore. When we were practicing the other day, it seemed as if we didn't even know each other."

"Oh," Mary-Kate said. "Yikes."

"I'm meeting Ross as soon as you and I are done with this painting stuff," Ashley said. "We're going to practice—big time. And when we're through, we'll be like *this*." She held out a hand with two of her fingers crossed. "Well, hopefully."

"I'm sure you guys will do fine," Mary-Kate said.

Suddenly Ashley's head jerked up. She pointed at the ceiling. "Listen," she whispered, staring at a vent high on the wall. "Can you hear that? Someone's talking up there."

Mary-Kate listened. "You're right!" she whispered back. "Where is that, anyway?"

Ashley frowned. "Wait here," she said quietly. She tiptoed into the hallway and gazed up the steps. Then she came back to the kitchen. "I think it's the girls' bathroom!" she announced.

Mary-Kate glanced toward the ceiling and nodded. Ashley was right. Someone in the girls' bathroom was talking—and the sound was carrying perfectly. If she and Ashley were quiet enough, they could hear every word!

"I can't believe it!" Mary-Kate whispered. "You know what this means, don't you?"

Ashley nodded, her eyes wide with alarm. "Miss Viola has probably heard every word we've ever said in the bathroom!"

Mary-Kate's mind raced. She was trying to remember every conversation she'd had in the bathroom. Had she ever said anything not so nice about

Miss Viola? Or . . . The Head? "Uh-oh. Remember that time we were complaining about—"

"Shh!" Ashley put a finger to her lips. "Listen." She pointed upward again.

Mary-Kate immediately recognized one of the voices. It was Dana!

"I can't believe this! It is *so* hilarious!" Dana was saying. "Can you believe she turned herself in?"

"I would *never* do that!" the other person said.

Mary-Kate glanced at Ashley. "Who is that?" she whispered.

"Kristen, I think," Ashley whispered back.

Upstairs, Dana and Kristen laughed.

"She's down there right now, painting all those cabinets!" Kristen said. "Maybe you should thank her."

"What for?" Dana asked.

"You *know* what for," Kristen said. *"You're* the one who left that window open and let the raccoon in."

"Hey, it wasn't my fault—I *had* to leave it open," Dana insisted. "What was I supposed to do? Sneak out at eleven to meet Nicholas—and take a chance that I couldn't get back in? You told me Miss Viola always checks the door before she goes to bed."

"True," Kristen agreed. "You had no choice."

"Besides," Dana said. "Mary-Kate will never find out."

Both girls giggled. Then someone turned on the water, and Mary-Kate couldn't hear anything else they said.

"I *knew* I didn't leave that stupid window open! And now I'm paying for something that Dana did!" Mary-Kate threw her paintbrush into the water can.

"I know," Ashley agreed, nodding. "It's awful."

Mary-Kate was so angry, she didn't know what to do. She just sat there on the floor, steaming.

The water went off upstairs. Mary-Kate and Ashley both looked toward the vent again and listened.

"So he and I are meeting at the Studio Arts Building at ten tonight," Dana said.

"Are you serious?" Kristen asked. "Mrs. Pritchard will be watching the dorms like a hawk!"

Dana giggled. "I doubt it. Not since Mary-Kate confessed! Besides, we have to talk about Nicholas's plan to make sure we win the Dream Date Debate." Dana's voice trailed off and disappeared as the two girls left the bathroom.

"Rats," Ashley said. "They're gone."

Mary-Kate sighed and picked up her paintbrush again. The sooner she and her sister finished, the better.

"How could Dana do that to you?" Ashley cried. "That is so low—even for her."

"No kidding," Mary-Kate said. "But I don't have to let her get away with it. I'm going to find out Dana's secret plan. And then I'm going to bust her for it!"

CHAPTER SIX

"So go ahead. Ask me anything!" Ross said to Ashley that night in the Student U. It was pretty empty for a Tuesday night. There were only three kids hanging out across the room, playing darts. A girl was sprawled out on the rug, reading.

"Now you're talking!" Ashley said. "I'm so glad that you're up for practicing."

"Of course I am," Ross replied. "I'm dying for us to win the date of your dreams." He fell into a bean-bag chair.

"Then you'll be really excited to see my chart," Ashley said.

"Chart?" Ross repeated.

"Yeah," Ashley said. "I made it after school." She

whipped out a color-coded piece of paper. "See? I divided the chart into categories. These are all the kinds of questions they might ask us at the Dream Date."

"Ooo-kay." Ross slowly nodded.

Ashley pointed to each color-coded section as she spoke. "There are also subsections. I wanted to be really specific. That way, there won't be anything about each other that we don't know."

Ashley glanced at Ross. He was staring at her poster with his mouth open. *He must be totally in awe of my amazing chart,* she thought.

"Um, Ashley," Ross said. "Don't you think this is all a little . . . much?"

"Of course not!" Ashley said. "We want to win, right? And this is how we'll do it!"

And then I won't have to worry about whether I know my boyfriend anymore, she added silently.

"I also made us a practice schedule." Ashley reached into her backpack and pulled out a calendar. "How about if we meet tomorrow night at six and Thursday right after school? And then we can meet again Friday morning really early. Before breakfast maybe. And we can spend all Friday night studying, too."

"Are you kidding me?" Ross threw up his hands.

"That's practically every single free minute between now and Saturday!"

"Exactly," Ashley said. "We need to maximize our practice time."

Ross sighed. "Ashley, I'm not too sure about this."

"Come on," Ashley said cheerfully. "Studying will be fun! I'll show you, okay? Pick a question."

"All right," Ross said, squinting at the chart. "Am I a morning person or a night person?"

Ashley thought for a second. "Morning?" she guessed.

"Yup!" Ross replied.

Ashley grinned. "Cool! Ask me another one."

Ross looked at the chart again. "Would I rather rent a movie or go to see it in the movie theater?" he asked.

"You would definitely go to the theater," Ashley said. She and Ross went to see movies all the time!

"Not really," Ross replied. "I'd rather rent. That way, I can replay the good parts!"

Ashley snapped her fingers. "Darn. I thought I had that one!" she said. "What's next?"

"My favorite dessert," Ross said.

"After lunch or after dinner?" Ashley asked.

"Are you serious?" Ross laughed. "Next you'll

45

be breaking down my favorite foods from each of the four basic food groups."

Ashley frowned. Ross wasn't taking this seriously. "Well, why not? Don't you want to win this thing?" she shot back.

"Hey, Ashley!" a voice interrupted them.

Ashley turned around. Phoebe had just walked into the Student U.

"What's up, Phoebe?" Ashley called.

Phoebe perched on the edge of a nearby table. "I looked through my closet again like you asked. It turns out that I have a pair of old boots that might work for your Paul Revere report."

"That's awesome!" Ashley cried. "Now I have my three articles of clothing!" She turned to Ross. "By the way, did you remember to bring that belt for me?"

"Oh, right." Ross rubbed his forehead. "I forgot it. Sorry."

Ashley raised her eyebrows. Ross had a great memory. In the whole time she had known him, he had never forgotten to do *anything*!

"You forgot it?" Ashley repeated. "But you promised me you'd bring it."

"Listen, Ashley," Ross replied, sounding annoyed. "I said I was sorry."

"Okay," Ashley said quickly. "I was just saying that you're always so responsible."

Ross looked away. "No, I'm not," he said. "You must not know me as well as you thought you did."

Ashley felt stung. How could Ross say that?

"Look, I don't feel like practicing anymore tonight," Ross said. "I'll see you tomorrow, okay?" He grabbed his backpack and left the Student U.

"What was *that* all about?" Phoebe said.

"I have no idea," Ashley said, staring after him. But one thing was really clear. The Dream Date Debate was turning into a dream date disaster!

CHAPTER SEVEN

As soon as Campbell started snoring after lights out that night, Mary-Kate got up from her bed. She was already dressed in black jeans and a sweatshirt.

She moved toward the door, trying hard not to wake Campbell. She didn't want her roommate to know that she was sneaking out to meet Jordan.

The hall was dark, but Mary-Kate could see moonlight streaming in from the windows downstairs. She shivered a little with excitement. Meeting Jordan under the starry sky was going to be totally romantic.

She was so glad he hadn't been mad about them missing the whole Dream Date deal. And he'd even offered to help her bust Dana and Nicholas.

Jordan was just . . . the best!

Mary-Kate quietly opened the window beside the front door to climb out. Then she turned around to make sure the window was closed—*all the way.*

No raccoon is going to get in this time! she thought.

She hurried across campus to the statue, where Jordan said he'd meet her.

He was sitting on the base of the statue already, wearing dark jeans, like Mary-Kate, and a hooded Harrington jacket. He jumped up as soon as he saw her coming.

"Hi," Mary-Kate said, shivering again.

"Hi." He smiled at her and took her hand. "Are you ready for this?"

Mary-Kate nodded. "What time is it?" she asked him. "Dana said she was meeting Nicholas at ten."

"It's a quarter till," Jordan said. "Listen, I scoped out the place already. I think we can hide in the shrubs next to the building. We'll have a good view and be able to hear them, too."

"Good idea," Mary-Kate said, nodding.

Mary-Kate and Jordan walked in silence until they reached the Studio Arts Building. Then they sat side by side against the wall, hidden behind a row of hedges.

"What time is it now?" Mary-Kate asked.

"Almost ten," Jordan replied.

Mary-Kate peeked around the corner at the steps of the building. Dana and Nicholas were nowhere in sight.

What if they don't show up? Mary-Kate wondered. *What if Jordan and I end up just sitting here in the dark? All alone?*

That would be . . . so romantic! But scary, too.

"Do you think maybe they're not coming?" Mary-Kate whispered after a while.

"I sort of hope they don't," he said, looking into her eyes. "It's cool just hanging out here with you."

Whoa! That's way romantic, Mary-Kate thought. She got that fluttering feeling in her stomach. She really, really wanted Jordan to kiss her. Almost without thinking, she began to lean forward.

But as soon as she did, Jordan drew back a little.

He's just as nervous as I am! Mary-Kate realized. She tried to think of something else to say but couldn't.

Jordan suddenly reached out and put an arm around her shoulders. Mary-Kate turned her face slightly toward him.

He's going to kiss me! she thought dreamily. *Finally!*

But just then she heard footsteps clicking on the path. Someone was coming! Mary-Kate turned her head toward the noise. Jordan quickly pulled away.

"Shh," he whispered softly. "There they are!"

Mary-Kate looked toward the spot where the sounds were coming from. Dana was just reaching the front of the Studio Arts Building. Nicholas was already there, waiting.

"So, did you bring it?" Dana asked.

"Yeah. It's in my backpack," Nicholas said.

Dana and Nicholas climbed the steps of the building and sat down. The moonlight was shining right on them, so Mary-Kate could see them both really well.

I hope they can't see us, she thought.

Very quietly, the two of them edged forward, being careful to stay in the shadow of the building.

They could see Dana and Nicholas perfectly. And luckily, sound carried easily in the crisp night air.

"How does it work?" Dana was asking Nicholas.

"I'll show you," Nicholas said. He pulled a couple of small items out of his backpack. "You wear this little gizmo in your ear. It's got a small wireless receiver built into it. Your hair will cover the whole thing."

"Let me try it." Dana took the gadget from him and put it in her ear.

What's going on? Mary-Kate wondered. She shot

51

Jordan a questioning glance, but he just shrugged.

"Perfect," Nicholas said. "So during the Dream Date Debate, we'll be able to give each other the right answers from behind the curtain."

Huh? Wait a minute, Mary-Kate thought. *Giving answers?*

Dana and Nicholas were planning to cheat!

Mary-Kate glanced at Jordan again and shook her head.

Jordan nodded silently and rolled his eyes. He obviously thought the same thing as Mary-Kate. Dana and Nicholas were both total creeps.

"Cool," Dana said. "But this thing better work."

"Let's test it out," Nicholas said. "I'll need to turn up the volume on your earpiece first."

"Why?" Dana asked as she handed it to him. "I can hear you fine."

"Because I'll have to whisper the answers while I'm backstage," Nicholas explained. "Otherwise, someone might hear me."

"Oh," Dana said. "Right."

Nicholas fiddled with the earpiece and handed it back to her. Next he clipped a small microphone to his collar. Then he stood up and walked about twenty feet away.

From the bushes, Mary-Kate couldn't hear what

he said next. But she could tell he was whispering something into the tiny microphone.

"Yup, I heard you," Dana called. "It works."

"Excellent," Nicholas said.

Dana laughed and tossed her long dark hair over her shoulders. "We are *so* going to win this thing," she said.

Mary-Kate wanted to scream. "I can't believe them!" she whispered angrily.

"Me, neither," Jordan said. "I feel like running out there and telling them off right now!"

"I know." Mary-Kate nodded. "But how are we going to prove anything? I mean, if we tell Mrs. Pritchard about any of this, it will be our word against theirs."

"And we'll get busted for sneaking out again," Jordan pointed out.

"Totally." Mary-Kate sighed. "But we can't let them get away with this."

"Don't worry—we won't," Jordan said.

"We won't?" Mary-Kate asked.

"Nope," Jordan said with a grin. "I have a plan to catch those cheaters red-handed!"

CHAPTER EIGHT

"Phoebe, I'm really getting nervous," Ashley said Thursday morning as they walked out of history class.

"How come?" Phoebe asked.

"You heard Mr. Montgomery today," Ashley said. "This project counts for a really big part of our grade. What if I mess up?"

"You won't, Ashley," Phoebe said. "You're almost done with your report, right? And you already have two pieces of clothing."

"I guess so," Ashley said. "I hope Ross brought the belt to school today like he said he would. He forgot *again* yesterday."

Plus he's been acting so weird, she added to herself.

It seemed as though Ross was almost trying to avoid her. Was he mad about that Dream Date stuff? She hoped not. They hardly had any time left to practice.

"Well, now's your chance to ask him about the belt," Phoebe said. "There he is!" She pointed down the hallway. Ross was standing outside a classroom, talking to some of his buddies.

"Cool," Ashley said. "See you later, Phoebe."

Phoebe waved and walked away.

Ashley took a deep breath and went up to her boyfriend. "Hi, Ross."

"Hey," Ross said. He nodded good-bye to his friends and turned back to Ashley. "What's up?"

"Well . . . I was just wondering if you brought the belt with you today," Ashley replied.

Ross slapped his head. "Oh, man! I forgot again. Can you believe it? Sorry."

Why am I not surprised? she thought. In fact, if she hadn't been seeing Ross for so long, she'd think he was forgetting on purpose!

"No, I can't believe it," Ashley told him. She put one hand on her hip. "You know how important this project is to me. How could you forget three days in a row?"

Ross wouldn't look at Ashley. "Well, I didn't

really forget. It's just . . . I couldn't get down to the basement last night. The door was locked."

Ashley narrowed her eyes. She had a feeling Ross wasn't telling the truth. "Couldn't you get someone to unlock the door?" she asked.

Ross didn't answer. He looked away as if he didn't want to talk about it.

I might not know my boyfriend as well as I thought I did, Ashley said to herself. *But I can definitely tell when he's hiding something*.

"Did you not bring the belt because you're mad at me?" Ashley asked.

"No, of course not," Ross said quickly.

"Then, what is it?" Ashley cried. "First you act all weird the past couple of days. And now you're lying to me—I can tell. What is going on?"

"Okay, okay." Ross glanced nervously around the hallway. "I'll tell you." He led her over to an empty corner.

Ashley was starting to get concerned. "Is everything okay?" she asked.

"Well, yeah," Ross said. "Sort of. I didn't want to tell you this. It's top secret. But I don't want you to be mad at me."

Top secret, Ashley thought. She wasn't expecting this! "What is it?" she asked.

Ross sighed. "Okay," he said. "Here goes." He was speaking so low that Ashley could barely hear him. "I'm afraid of spiders."

"Huh?" Ashley jerked her head back and stared at him. "What does *that* have to do with anything?"

"That's why I didn't bring you the belt," Ross said. "It's in the basement, and I can't go down there to get it."

Ashley had to think for a moment before she understood. "Ohhhhh. You mean there are spiders in the basement of your dorm?" she said.

"Shh!" Ross glanced around again to see if anyone was listening. "Yes," he whispered. "Tons of them. I tried to go down there to get the belt for you, but I freaked out. Spiders are, like, my biggest fear."

Wow, Ashley thought. *I never knew Ross was afraid of spiders!*

But then again she wasn't really surprised. At this point there were a million things she didn't know about him!

"Don't worry," Ashley said. "Everyone is afraid of *something*. I'm *totally* afraid of hat hair," she joked.

Ross laughed. "Well, just don't tell anyone about this, okay?" he said. "It's . . . embarrassing."

"I won't tell," Ashley promised. "But, hey, it's no big deal. Maybe one of your friends could go down to the basement and get the belt for me."

Ross shook his head. "No way. They'd want to know why, and I'd have to tell them. And then I'd never live it down. Everyone would think I was a major wuss."

Ashley nodded. She understood how Ross felt. She wished with all her heart that she could help him get over his fear so he wouldn't be embarrassed.

"I'm really sorry, Ashley," Ross said. "It's too bad girls aren't allowed in the dorm. Otherwise you could go down to the basement yourself."

"No problem," Ashley said. "It's okay." But inside, she was starting to panic. If Ross didn't give her the buckle, where was she going to find a third piece of Paul Revere-type clothing? She had to hand it in with her report on Monday!

There was only one thing to do. She had to come up with a plan to cure Ross of his fear of spiders.

But how?

"Remember—you promised not to tell *anyone* about this spider deal," Ross said.

Ashley crossed her heart with one finger. "Don't worry, Ross. My lips are sealed."

CHAPTER NINE

"*Think*, Mary-Kate," Ashley said. "There has to be a way to help a person get over a fear of spiders."

"So who is this person, anyway?" Mary-Kate asked, flopping onto her bed.

Who? I can't tell you that, Ashley thought. *Ross would never forgive me!*

"No one you know," Ashley fibbed. "Just some guy I met in the Harrington library."

"So why do you have to help him get over his fear?" Mary-Kate asked.

"Ummm . . . " Ashley thought fast. She was making this whole story up as she went along. She didn't want to blow Ross's secret.

"Because he's going on a camping trip next

59

week," she said. "I feel really bad for him. So I told him I would try to think of something."

"Well, I read in a magazine once that if you want to get over a fear, you're supposed to face it a little at a time," Mary-Kate said.

"Really?" Ashley asked. That sounded like a good idea.

"Yeah," Mary-Kate said. "That way, you get used to the fear and find out it's not as bad as you thought it was."

"So I should make him face spiders a few at a time?" Ashley said slowly.

"I guess." Mary-Kate shrugged.

Ashley leaned back against Mary-Kate's bed. "So will you help me?" she asked.

"Help? How?" Mary-Kate tossed a tennis ball against the wall.

"Go out in the woods for me and get the spiders," Ashley said. "You know you're braver about that stuff than I am."

Mary-Kate rolled her eyes. "You can't just go out in the woods and *get* spiders," she said. "Besides— some of them are poisonous. It's not a good idea."

"Well, you suggested it," Ashley said.

"I didn't mean *real* spiders," Mary-Kate said. "I was thinking of fake ones. Campbell has this whole box of tiny rubber spiders under her bed. They were a big hit at Halloween."

"Hmmm," Ashley said, thinking. "I could invite this guy on a picnic. And secretly plant the rubber spiders in his food. When he sees them, maybe he'll get over his fear."

"Sounds like a plan to me," Mary-Kate said.

"Do you think I could borrow Campbell's spiders?" Ashley said.

"Sure, she won't mind," Mary-Kate replied. She got up and reached under her roommate's bed. Then she pulled out a box and tossed it to Ashley.

Ashley opened the box and peered inside. It was filled to the brim with wiggly rubber spiders!

"Excellent!" Ashley said. "Thanks, Mary-Kate. You saved my life."

Mary-Kate looked confused. "Why?" she said. "What does this have to do with you?"

Oops! Ashley grabbed the spiders and left the room before her sister could ask any more questions!

The next day at lunchtime Ashley fixed a special picnic for herself and Ross. It had tons of treats—all the things Ross liked to eat.

How many spiders should I use? Ashley wondered as she put together the basket.

61

Mary-Kate had said to use a couple of spiders at a time. But Ashley was on a tight schedule. The report was due on Monday!

I'm sure Ross will be able to handle it if I add a few more, Ashley told herself. She dumped the entire box of spiders in the picnic basket.

She sprinkled some in the bag of popcorn.

She stuck one on top of a blueberry muffin. She tucked another inside a candy bar wrapper.

Just for good measure, she put a few in the rolled-up napkins.

That should do it, Ashley thought with satisfaction. She grabbed the basket and hurried to meet Ross outside the Student U.

The sun was shining and it was almost warm. A nice day for a picnic!

"Hi," Ross said when Ashley arrived. "I brought a blanket."

"Perfect," Ashley said. "Are you hungry?"

"Definitely," Ross replied. "I've been eating stewed tomatoes in the dining hall all week!"

"Well, you're in luck," Ashley said. "There are no stewed tomatoes in this basket." She sat down and held out a blueberry muffin and smiled at the cute little rubber spider stuck on top.

I hope this works! she thought.

Ross took the muffin without looking and started to peel the paper off.

"So, do you want to practice for Dream Date again?" Ross asked. "We have only one day left."

"You bet," Ashley said, glad that he wanted to start practicing again. But first things first. She stared at the muffin, waiting for him to notice the spider.

"Okay, ask me a question," Ross said just as he was about to take a bite of the muffin.

Then he saw it.

"Ahhhh!" he screamed, throwing the muffin down. It landed on Ashley's lap.

"What are *those*?" Ross cried, pointing to the spiders in the popcorn.

Ashley didn't have a chance to answer.

"Ahhhh!" Ross shouted, smacking the popcorn away. It flew all over the place. The spiders did, too.

"Get those things out of here!" Ross yelled.

"It's okay," Ashley told him quickly. "They're just rubber. See?" She grabbed the muffin and a few other rubber spiders to show him.

Ross stared at her for a moment. He glanced at the rubber spiders, then back at Ashley. "Whoa, wait a second," he said, shaking his head. "You mean you actually did this on *purpose*?"

"Well, yes," Ashley said. "I was trying to—"

"Are you nuts?" Ross cried. "I tell you my deepest, darkest secret—and you throw it back in my face?"

"No!" Ashley shook her head quickly. "I wasn't trying to make fun of you. I was trying to help."

Ross folded his arms and glared at her.

"Really!" Ashley said. "I thought this would help you get over your fear."

"Well, it won't," Ross said. "So *don't* do it again."

"Okay," Ashley said in a small voice. "Sorry, Ross." She felt really bad. The last thing she wanted to do was freak Ross out even more. "I'll get us some drinks, okay?"

She ran into the Student U and bought two sodas. By the time she got back, Ross had opened one of the sandwiches Ashley had brought.

"Do you want peanut butter and jelly?" Ross asked. He held out the sandwich and smiled.

"Sure, thanks," Ashley said, glad to see that he was in a better mood.

She took the sandwich and started to bite into it but then saw something on the edge of the bread.

A little black spider.

"Ha-ha. Very funny," Ashley said. She flicked the spider off her sandwich. It flew onto Ross's arm.

The spider began to move. Ashley watched, horrified, as it began to crawl up Ross's sleeve.

That spider wasn't rubber. It was *real*!

"Auuuggghhh!" Ross yelled. He jumped up and brushed the spider off his arm as fast as he could.

"Ohmigosh!" Ashley cried. "I'm sorry! I'm sorry!"

"What is the matter with you?" Ross shouted. "Are you trying to give me a heart attack or something?"

"No, I . . . " Ashley began.

But Ross was steaming mad. "That's it!" he said. "I'm finished with this stupid picnic. And I don't want to hang out with *you* for a while, either."

He grabbed his backpack.

"Ross, wait!" Ashley cried. "What about the Dream Date?"

"Forget it," Ross yelled. "I'm not going." Then he stormed away.

Ashley didn't know what to do. She had never seen Ross so angry! And instead of helping, she'd made things even worse. Now she didn't have the buckle for her report. She didn't have a partner for the Dream Date. And worst of all, she didn't know if she had a boyfriend anymore!

CHAPTER
TEN

"What am I going to do?" Ashley moaned. "Ross isn't speaking to me. He wouldn't even read the note I gave him yesterday afternoon."

Ashley pulled her knees up on the chair. She and Mary-Kate were sitting in the lounge at Porter House. It was early Saturday afternoon—the day of the Dream Date Debate.

This was supposed to be my big day, Ashley thought. *Ross and I were going to show everyone we're the perfect couple!*

"What did the note say?" Mary-Kate asked.

"It was really nice," Ashley replied. "I told him that I was sorry about the spiders. And that I really didn't know that the spider I flicked on him was real. And I apologized about the Dream Date, too. I said I knew I'd been way too pushy. I even said it didn't matter about that stupid buckle!"

"Ross didn't read the note at all?" Mary-Kate asked.

Ashley shook her head.

"Did he throw it away?"

"No, he stuffed it in his backpack," Ashley said. "And when I tried to talk to him after class, he wouldn't speak to me."

"Wow," Mary-Kate said. "Sounds serious."

"And now I won't have the third thing I need for my Paul Revere report, either," Ashley added. "I'll probably get an F, but who cares. I just want Ross to forgive me."

"Bummer," Mary-Kate said.

Ashley turned to her sister. "Isn't this the worst?" she said. "We thought at least *one* of us was going to win the Dream Date."

"I know," Mary-Kate said, sighing. "Oh, well."

"Hey, what about Dana and Nicholas?" Ashley asked. Mary-Kate had told her about their plan to cheat at the Dream Date. "Are you and Jordan still going to bust them?"

Mary-Kate's eyes danced. "Wait and see," she said. "We have a really cool plan to catch them in the act. Just keep your fingers crossed and hope it works!"

"I'll cross all ten fingers," Ashley said. She twisted her fingers, trying to do it. "The only thing that could possibly make me feel worse than I do now is if Dana wins the game!"

"I'd better go meet Jordan." Mary-Kate headed for the door. "See you over at Harrington?"

Ashley nodded. "I'll be there." *All by myself,* she added miserably.

Ashley changed her clothes and caught the next shuttle bus to Harrington. She slipped into the auditorium and looked around.

The place was buzzing. Samantha and Nathan were still going over questions from last year's list. Other teams hung out in the hallway, chatting and laughing.

If only Ross were here, Ashley thought. *At least we could watch the game together.* She took a seat in the fourth row and waited for everyone else to come in.

A few guys were setting up a backdrop on the stage. Mrs. Pritchard was directing them where to place it.

"Isn't this cool?" Phoebe said as she passed Ashley. "I love the vintage set!"

Ashley nodded. The stage was set up to look like

a nineteen sixties game show. The backdrop had lots of swirls and hearts painted on it in zillions of colors. The words "Dream Date Debate" were painted in glittery blue.

Jennifer Brent was the game master. She sat at a small desk with a microphone at the front of the stage.

Six folding chairs were lined up in pairs at an angle beside the desk.

"Hi," a familiar voice said behind Ashley.

She whirled around. "Ross?"

Ashley was so happy to see him, she almost jumped out of her seat.

"I read your note," Ross said.

"You did?" Ashley's heart pounded in her chest. "I'm really sorry, Ross. About everything."

"It's okay," Ross went on. "I know you were just trying to help me with my spider fears. And guess what? It sort of worked."

"It did?" Ashley couldn't believe it.

"Well, not totally," Ross said. "I was really freaked when that spider was crawling up my arm, but after I had time to think about it, I sort of thought, 'Hey. No biggie.' So I went down to the basement last night and got the buckle."

He reached into his pocket and handed it to her.

"Oh, Ross, that's so sweet!" Ashley said. "And brave. I mean it. I'm totally impressed with you."

Ross shrugged. "Well, I didn't exactly go alone. I got my dorm master to go with me. And I'd still rather not hang out with any spiders. But I guess I can handle them if I have to."

"Thanks," Ashley said. "I bet I'll get an A on my project for sure now."

"So do you still want to be in this thing?" Ross nodded toward the stage.

"The Dream Date Debate?" Ashley could barely hide her excitement. "Definitely!" She leaped out of her seat. "And it's okay if we don't win. I just want us to have fun!"

"Welcome, First Formers, to your first Dream Date Debate," Mrs. Pritchard said from the stage.

All the kids in the audience began to clap and stomp their feet.

Mrs. Pritchard smiled. "Since we have quite a few couples entered, I'm going to turn things over right away to our game master, Jennifer Brent. Good luck, everyone!"

"They're starting!" Mary-Kate whispered to Jordan excitedly. The two of them stood in the wings backstage. By then, the auditorium was packed. Nearly every student from the Harrington and White Oak First Forms was there to watch.

"Cool," Jordan said. "I've got everything covered. Why don't you go out and sit in the audience?"

"Okay." Mary-Kate nodded. She giggled to herself as she tried to find a seat. Their plan was brilliant! And simple.

Jordan was going to hang around backstage while Dana and Nicholas played the game. As soon as Nicholas started whispering the answers to Dana into his microphone, Jordan would sneak up on him—and grab the microphone away!

Mary-Kate chuckled to herself. Jordan was going to yell "Cheater! Cheater!" into the microphone. She couldn't wait.

There was a seat one row behind Mrs. Pritchard. Mary-Kate quickly slid in.

Jennifer called the first three couples onstage. "In round one, we have Wendy and Jeff, Brooke and D.J., and Dana and Nicholas," she announced.

"Okay, you know how this works," Jennifer told the audience. "I'm going to send the guys backstage first. While they're gone, I'll ask the girls some questions. The girls will write the answers down on these." Jennifer held up some big yellow cards. "Then we'll bring the guys back out," she went on. "I'll ask them the same questions. If a guy's answer matches the one his partner wrote down, their team gets a point. Then we'll reverse the game. The girls will go backstage and the guys will try to guess *their* answers."

Jennifer turned to the couples onstage. "Are our contestants ready?"

All of the couples nodded.

"Okay, then," Jennifer said. "Guys, Miss Viola will lead you backstage. Let the Dream Date Debate begin!"

The audience cheered and clapped again.

"Question number one, ladies," Jennifer began when everyone had settled down. "What is your partner's favorite TV show?"

Wendy and Brooke wrote down their answers right away.

Mary-Kate watched as Dana pretended to think.

I'll bet Nicholas is telling her the answer right now, Mary-Kate thought.

"Question number two," Jennifer announced. "If your partner could choose, would he rather go on a skiing vacation or hit the beach?"

Again, Wendy and Brooke wrote down their answers immediately.

Dana took her time. Then she wrote down her answer, too.

Oh, man, Mary-Kate thought. She wasn't sure how many questions there were. What if Jordan didn't get to Nicholas in time?

"Question number three. Name the food your partner hates the most," Jennifer said.

Wendy and Brooke both started writing. But Dana just sat there.

She looks like she's listening, Mary-Kate thought. *Or waiting for something. What's happening?*

All of a sudden, Dana jumped up and screamed. "Owww!" she cried. She yanked something out of her ear and threw it onto the stage.

"Excuse me," Mrs. Pritchard said, rising from her seat. "What on earth are you doing, Dana? Were you wearing an *earpiece*?"

Dana froze. "Ummm . . . " she said, looking down at the little piece of plastic on the floor.

"That's right," Mary-Kate said, jumping up behind Mrs. Pritchard. "She's totally cheating. Nicholas is feeding her answers from backstage!"

Some of the kids in the audience gasped. Everyone started talking at once.

"Quiet, people!" Mrs. Pritchard said, hushing the crowd. "Dana—is this true?"

Dana didn't answer. But the curtains onstage started moving. A moment later Jordan pushed his

73

way through them onto the stage. He was waving the small microphone in the air.

"Yeah, it's true," Jordan said. "I caught Nicholas with this microphone backstage."

The students in the audience started mumbling and talking again.

"Quiet, please," Mrs. Pritchard told them. "Dana, this is inexcusable. Where's Nicholas?"

A Harrington teacher went backstage and found Nicholas. He brought him onto the stage.

Nicholas looked really nervous.

"This behavior is *not* in the spirit of White Oak *or* Harrington," Mrs. Pritchard said sternly. "I'm afraid you two will have to withdraw from the game. Please go back to your dorms. I'll speak to you later about your punishment."

Yes! Mary-Kate thought. That's exactly what those cheating creeps deserved! She spotted Ashley on the side of the stage and shot her a triumphant smile.

"Mrs. Pritchard?" Jennifer Brent said from the stage. "What about the game? We need three couples for each round."

Mary-Kate's eyes grew wide. She knew who that third couple could be!

"Mrs. Pritchard?" Mary-Kate said, stepping forward. "Could Jordan and I take Dana's place in the game? We really wanted to play."

Mrs. Pritchard didn't answer right away. She looked from Mary-Kate to Jordan, then back at Mary-Kate.

Oh, please! Mary-Kate thought. *Please. It would be so much fun!*

"All right, Mary-Kate," Mrs. Pritchard said. "Under the circumstances, you and Jordan may take Dana and Nicholas's place in the game."

"Thank you, Mrs. Pritchard!" Mary-Kate cried. She hurried up to the stage. She and Jordan were going to be in the Dream Date Debate after all!

CHAPTER ELEVEN

Ashley was so happy for her sister, she cheered. "Yay, Mary-Kate!" she called out.

She turned to Ross, who was beside her. They were standing in the wings, waiting for their turn to go on.

"Isn't that great?" Ashley said.

"Totally!" Ross agreed.

"Okay, let's settle down, please," Mrs. Pritchard said. "Jennifer, why don't you read all three questions again for Mary-Kate? She can write down her answers. Then we'll go on with the rest of the questions."

Ashley moved to the side of the stage so she could peek around the curtain.

When Mary-Kate had finished all her answers, the three guys came back out. Jordan, Jeff, and D.J.

"Okay, we'll start with Wendy and Jeff," Jennifer said. "Question number one: Jeff, what's your favorite TV show?"

"Easy," Jeff said. *"The Simpletons."*

"Yes!" Wendy cried, holding up her first yellow card. She had written THE SIMPLETONS on it with a big black marker.

"Okay," Jennifer said. "That's one point for Wendy and Jeff."

"Go, Wendy!" someone called from the audience.

Then Jennifer read the next question. "If you could go on a skiing vacation or hit the beach, which one would you pick?"

"Skiing," Jeff said.

"Yee-ha!" Wendy shouted as she held up her second card.

Everyone in the audience laughed.

"Two points for your team," Jennifer said.

The audience clapped. Someone gave a long, screeching whistle.

One by one, Jennifer went through all the questions. Wendy and Jeff did pretty well. They got four questions right. Brooke and D.J. did terribly. They didn't get *any* right!

How embarrassing! Ashley thought. *I hope that doesn't happen to Ross and me.* She held her breath when it was Mary-Kate's turn to show her answers.

"Okay, Jordan," Jennifer said. "First question: What's your favorite TV show?"

"Extreme Sports," Jordan said.

Mary-Kate held up her yellow card. She had written EXTREME SPORTS on it.

"Way to go, Mary-Kate!" Ashley cheered.

"Question two: Jordan, what would you choose? Skiing or the beach?" Jennifer asked.

Mary-Kate got that one right, too.

By the time they were done, Mary-Kate had gotten all five questions right!

Then the teams switched and the boys answered questions about the girls. Jordan got all the answers right, too!

"They totally won that round," Ashley said, nudging Ross. "Isn't that great?"

"Let's hope we do that well," he said. He sounded a little worried.

"Hey, whatever happens is fine with me," Ashley said. She was just thrilled to be back in the game. And even happier that Ross wasn't mad at her anymore. "Come on—it's our turn," she said eagerly when the first round was over.

Ashley's stomach did a little flip-flop when she took a seat onstage. But she really wasn't worried.

Sure, it would be great to win, she thought. *But it's more important that things are cool with Ross again.*

I just hope we get some of the questions right!

The round whizzed by quickly. To Ashley's surprise, the questions were easy. The first one was What's your favorite color?

Ashley knew the right answer, thanks to all their practicing. Red.

She aced three more questions—and missed on number five. Oh, well.

Ashley glanced at the competition. Summer and Dylan were the next team in this round. But so far they hadn't gotten a single question right!

"Okay, Dylan," Jennifer said. "Last chance. Question number five: Do you have any pets? If so, what kind of animal is it and what's its name?"

"I don't have any pets," Dylan said.

"Oh, yes, you do!" Summer said. Her eyes popped open wide. "You told me you have dust bunnies under your bed!"

Everyone in the audience roared with laughter.

"Um, let's see your answer," Jennifer said.

Summer blushed and held up her card. She had written "Dust Bunny—No Name" on it.

"Sorry," Jennifer said. "I can't give you any points for that."

The next couple was Elise and Peter Jacoby. They ended up with three points.

When the couples switched, Ross got all five questions right about Ashley. Peter got three questions right. But Dylan did just as well as Summer—he got zero!

"Ross, we won our round!" Ashley said excitedly. She gave him a quick hug.

"I guess all that crazy practicing paid off," Ross said with a laugh.

Ashley nodded. She couldn't believe they were going to the final round. "We could still win the dream date!"

"Cool," Ross said.

Ashley glanced at him sideways. He actually looked excited!

Then Ashley started thinking about the romantic restaurant again. The horse-drawn carriage. The fancy dinner. Maybe she'd wear her black dress and silver shawl. . . .

She and Ross watched the third round from the audience. Samantha and Nathan won easily.

Then it was time for the final round with Mary-Kate's, Ashley's, and Samantha's teams. The boys answered questions first. All three teams got four points!

"This is so close!" Ashley squealed as the boys went backstage. "Good luck," she said to Mary-Kate and Samantha as the three of them took their seats onstage.

"Thanks," Mary-Kate said, smiling. "You, too."

"Yeah, good luck to all of us!" Samantha said.

"Okay, this is it," Jennifer announced. "For the big prize—the dream date! Question number one: If your partner could eat only one food for a week, would he choose pizza or hamburgers?"

I know he'd pick pizza over candy, Ashley told herself. *But would he choose pizza over burgers? Hmmm . . .*

"Question number two," Jennifer began.

"Wait!" Ashley blurted out. "I'm not ready."

Everyone in the audience laughed.

"Well, hurry up," Jennifer said, grinning.

Ashley scribbled "pizza" on the card and nodded. "Okay. Go ahead."

"Question number two: If your partner could live anywhere in the world, where would it be?" Jennifer asked.

That one's a piece of cake, Ashley thought. Ross had always said he wanted to learn to surf and live in Hawaii.

Questions three and four were a cinch, too. Ashley knew the answers for sure. She was starting to get excited now. They really had a chance to win the game!

Then she heard Jennifer read the next question.

"Question number five: What is your partner's biggest fear?"

Ashley froze. Oh, *no!* This was it. The one question she didn't want to answer.

Her heart started pounding. *What should I do?* she wondered.

She and Ross were doing so well. The big prize was practically theirs.

But I can't tell everybody that Ross is afraid of spiders, Ashley thought. *I promised.*

"Come on, Ashley. Time's almost up," Jennifer said. "Write down your answer."

Ashley swallowed hard. *I can't do this to Ross*, she decided finally. *I'll have to make something up.*

She wrote the word "vampires" on her card.

When the guys came out, everyone started cheering. Ashley twisted her hands in her lap. Had she done the right thing?

Samantha and Nathan went first. They got only three questions right.

"France?" Nathan said when he heard Samantha's

answer to question number two. "What makes you think I'd *ever* want to live there?"

Samantha blushed. "I guess that's where *I* want to live," she admitted.

"Well, *bon voyage*," Nathan joked. The audience laughed.

Mary-Kate and Jordan went next. They did really well. They got all five questions right!

Oh, wow, Ashley thought. Ross and I have to get them all right, too—just to tie!

Jennifer read the first four questions to Ross. Ashley's answers matched Ross's perfectly.

Then it was time for the final question.

"Okay, folks. Mary-Kate and Jordan are ahead with five points," Jennifer announced. "So far, Ashley and Ross have four. If Ashley and Ross get the next one right, we'll have a tie."

Ashley squeezed her eyes shut tightly. *Please, please, let Ross say vampires,* she begged silently.

"And if there is a tie," Jennifer went on, "*both* couples will get to go on a dream date."

"What if we don't get the answer right?" Ross asked.

"Then Mary-Kate and Jordan will win," Jennifer said, shrugging. "Okay, final question for the grand prize. Ross, what is your biggest fear?"

Ross shot Ashley a smile. "That's easy," he answered. "Spiders. I'm really afraid of spiders."

Ashley's shoulders slumped. She never thought he'd let everybody know his deepest, darkest secret!

"And what did you write on the card, Ashley?" Jennifer asked.

Ashley held it up. "I wrote 'vampires,'" she said. "I guess I don't know as much about Ross as I thought."

Ross tilted his head a little in surprise. He stared at Ashley.

"So Mary-Kate and Jordan are our big winners!" Jennifer announced. The audience clapped and whistled.

Mary-Kate jumped up from her chair and gave Jordan a hug. "Wow!" she said. "We won! We really won!"

"Congratulations," Ashley said to her sister, smiling. She was really happy for Mary-Kate. "Good game."

"Yeah, thanks," Mary-Kate said. "You guys did a great job, too."

Ashley pulled Ross into the wings, where no one could see them. "How come you told the truth about the spiders?" she asked softly. "I thought you didn't want anyone to know."

"I wanted to win the game," he said, taking her hand. "For you."

Wow, Ashley thought. *That is so sweet!*

"But we didn't win—because you lied to protect me," Ross said.

Ashley nodded. "I'd never give away your secret," she told him. "That's a lot more important than anything else."

"Cool," Ross said. He squeezed her hand. "Well, I'm sorry we lost. I know you really wanted to go on that big date."

The fancy restaurant would have been romantic, all right, Ashley thought. But nothing could be better than this. Having her boyfriend do something so sweet and unselfish—just for her.

"I don't mind," Ashley said. "Mary-Kate and Jordan will have an awesome time alone together on their dream date."

"No, we won't," Mary-Kate said, coming up to them.

"You won't?" Ashley said, turning to her sister. "Why not?"

"Because we want the pizza party," Mary-Kate announced. "You guys are invited, of course. And so are all the other couples from the contest! So *everybody* wins!"

• • •

Ashley and Mary-Kate walked to the pizza party together the next Saturday night. The moon wasn't full, but it was bright. And the sky was full of shining stars.

Mary-Kate was wearing new jeans and her favorite green top with a boat neckline. Ashley wore a purple dress that laced up the front and had a ruffle along the hem.

"Hey, I heard about your Paul Revere report," Mary-Kate said. "Congratulations. Phoebe told me you got an A."

"Yup," Ashley said. "Thanks to her and Ross."

"Well, at least now you can totally relax and enjoy yourself tonight," Mary-Kate said.

"Mmm," Ashley replied as they stepped into the Student U. "So how come you chose the party?"

"Because this is so much better!" Mary-Kate looked around. "My favorite So So So CD is playing, and the pizzas smell yummy, and . . . "

Jordan suddenly came up and started to pull Mary-Kate away. "Come on, let's dance," he said. "It's a slow song, though. Is that okay?"

"See what I mean?" Mary-Kate called to Ashley over her shoulder.

Jordan put his arms around Mary-Kate when

they reached the dance floor. "Maybe this can be our song," he said.

Mary-Kate nodded. "Maybe we'll hear it at the concert," she said.

Jordan smiled at her the whole time they danced. It felt great to be so close to him. But when the song ended, he motioned toward the video game room.

"Hey, they got Kung Fu Cooks in," he said. "You want to play?"

"Sure," Mary-Kate said.

Jordan took her hand and led her to the small back room, where the video games were. But when they got there, the room was empty.

Jordan turned to face her. "You look great," he said softly.

Mary-Kate's heart started thumping. She had a feeling something very special was about to happen.

He leaned forward as if he was going to kiss her. But just then Nathan Berger came into the room.

"Whoa! Look what I found!" Nathan teased, laughing. "Our dream couple!"

Jordan pulled away for a second.

Oh, no! Not again! Mary-Kate thought. *Every time he tries to kiss me, something interrupts us!*

Jordan shot Nathan a glare. "Just get out of here, Berger, okay?" he said.

"No way." Nathan laughed, crossing his arms. "I don't want to miss this."

Jordan shrugged. "Yeah? Well, neither do I!"

He leaned over and kissed Mary-Kate.

It wasn't a long kiss, but it was really sweet.

Finally! Mary-Kate thought happily. Their first kiss!

She looked quickly over her shoulder. Nathan was gone.

"Now, this is my idea of a dream date," Jordan said, grinning.

Mine, too! Mary-Kate thought. *And if this date is really a dream—I hope it never ends!*

DREAM DATE FOR TWENTY
by Phoebe Cahill

The moon was bright last Saturday, and the night air was soft and breezy. In other words, it was the perfect evening for a romantic dream date for two. Or twenty!

Thanks to Mary-Kate and Jordan, the winners of the Dream Date Debate, there was a very special pizza party in the Student U for all the other contestants, plus a few more friends. (Talk about double-dating!)

Not everyone was with their dream date, though. Brooke Miller was totally grossed out when she noticed her date's retainer buried under the pile of toppings on her pizza slice. (On the flipside, D.J. Turner was really excited to find his retainer!)

Summer Sorenson and Dylan Tunnell spent the whole night going over Dream Date Debate questions, hoping they'd finally get at least one question right. (No such luck.)

Jeff Duncan stepped on Wendy Linden's toe so hard while they were dancing that Wendy had to stop and sit down. But she was so into the music that she couldn't stay still for long. In fact, she invented a new dance step. By the end of the night, everyone was doing—the Limp!

Party on, White Oak and Harrington!

GLAM GAB
TOP SIX SIGNS
THAT IT'S SPRING
by Ashley Burke

Fashion expert Ashley Burke

1. Jeff Morgan and Noah Simon traded in their grungy basketball jerseys for grungy baseball jerseys. (Hey, guys—how'd you get them so grungy this early in the season?)

2. Mrs. Pritchard finally stopped wearing her gray wool suit.

3. Instead of one inch of midriff showing above her jeans, Summer Sorensen is now going for two inches.

4. Phoebe Cahill decided it was warm enough to break out her vintage 1950s shortie pajamas at the slumber party in the lounge last Saturday night.

5. Ginger "Turn Up the Heat" Halliday actually shed her extra-padded down jacket!

6. Elise Van Hook broke out her Capri pants (so now we can see her sparkly socks)!

A SPORT FOR ALL SEASONS
by Mary-Kate Burke

Sports pro Mary-Kate Burke

Tired of playing the same old sports? Well, wake up, 'cause I've searched the globe for some new, exciting ones. They're kind of like the sports we play in the U.S.—with a fun twist!

The perfect sport for spring is Netball, which is played in countries like Canada. It's kind of like basketball—except when the players have the ball, they're not allowed to move!

Cricket is a fun sport for summer. It's played in Australia and England and resembles baseball. The big difference is the pitcher doesn't throw the ball to a catcher. The pitcher is aiming for two pieces of wood behind the batter, and if he hits them, the batter is out for the rest of the game!

The winter sport I found is my favorite. It's called Yukigassen, and it is played in Great Britain. It's kind of a cross between capture the flag and a snowball fight. Players try to capture the other team's flag, while everyone else hurls snowballs at them!

Want to find out more about these sports? The Internet has tons of info. Learn all the rules and get in on the action with your friends!

THE FIRST FORM BUZZ
by Dana Woletsky

Well, it's been a good month for gossip, with lots of people letting the cat out of the bag (and one person letting a raccoon in! But we'll get to that later.).

First question: How many White Oak girls does it take to unscrew a light bulb in the Student U? I heard the lights went out for a few minutes at the Dream Date pizza party.

But even in the dark, I hear that JM still didn't kiss MKB—or did he?

Second question: Why is AB spending so much time hanging around the used-clothing stores in town? I

thought vintage was her roomie's thing. Maybe AB is trying to match her honey's style—'cause we all know RL's wardrobe is hopelessly out of date!

Speaking of dates, is SK kidding herself or does she really think NB is her dream date? They sure have been spending a lot of time together. But if you ask me, he's more like a nightmare!

Now about that raccoon . . . no matter what MKB says, I still think she left the window open!

That's it for this month. Remember: If you want the scoop, you just gotta snoop!

THE GET-REAL GIRL

Dear Get-Real Girl,

I don't want to go home to L.A. for the summer. I'm going to miss my friends at White Oak too much! I know I can always call them on my cell phone (I get free long distance), but it just won't be the same. I'm so used to having them around all the time!

Signed,
Lonely in Los Angeles

Dear Lonely,

Just one question: Exactly how many free minutes do you have on that cell phone? (And can I borrow it?)

But seriously, I know it's hard to leave your friends— especially ones that you see every single day! But think of it this way: Now you'll have the chance to reunite with your friends from home! I guarantee that once you get there, you'll remember all the things you missed about your old neighborhood. And by the end of the summer, you'll probably be sad about leaving to come back here!

Signed,
Get-Real Girl

Dear Get-Real Girl,

I have a secret fear that no one knows about. I get totally grossed out when I see bare feet. And the worst part is, my room-mate puts her bare feet on my bed all the time! What should I do?

Signed,
Freaked by Feet

Dear Freaked,

Why not go ahead and tell your roomie about your problem? If you're honest, I'm sure she'll respect your wishes and keep her feet all covered up. But be careful with how you tell her. You don't want to put your foot in your mouth or anything. After all—that would *really* gross you out!

Signed,
Get-Real Girl

UPCOMING CALENDAR
Spring/Summer

Calling all cooks! (Except the real ones!) It's time to turn the tables—and the ovens—when White Oak girls cook a fancy dinner

for the dining-hall staff. Sign up by Friday and bring your best recipes. (No Mystery Meat allowed!)

Spring into spring with a schoolwide picnic on the lawn at Harrington, May 15. And just to keep up with the "springy" theme, Harrington will supply the

pogo sticks. Get ready to bounce!

Are summer-camp decisions cramping your style? Then check out the Camp Fair Jamboree at noon on May 20 in the auditorium. Camps from across the country will be there, including Camp Click, the photography camp, and the twin camps—Camp Hunnimuc and Munnihuc. (Try saying that three times fast!)

Worried about missing all the White Oak gossip while you're at the beach this summer? Then don't wave good-bye to your friends until you've signed up for the White Oak Summer E-mail Newsletter! Gossip has never been so hot and steamy!

IT'S ALL IN THE STARS
Spring Horoscopes

Taurus
(April 20-May 20)

Feeling clumsy these days? Sort of like a bull in a china shop? That can happen to Taurus the Bull every once in a while. Just hang in there and let the klutz factor pass. Pretty soon you'll be juggling all aspects of your life like a pro!

Gemini
(May 21-June 21)

Spring fever has hit, and suddenly you wish there were two of you—one Gemini to do all the studying for finals, and another Gemini to flirt with that new cute guy. Well, relax. There's plenty of time for everything if you pace yourself. With all your natural Gemini charms, you can study and flirt at the same time! (That cute guy goes to the library, doesn't he?)

Cancer
(June 22-July 21)

Knock, knock. Who's there? You are, of course—because Cancers are often happiest at home. But don't become too much of a homebody. Now is the time to get out and have some fun. How else are you going to meet that special friend who wants to spend the weekends just like you do—hanging out at home?

#29: Love-Set-Match

Dear Diary,

This is our most exciting summer yet! Mary-Kate and I have just arrived at camp. We're here without our friends, which means we're going to meet a whole new group of kids!

We even decided to try stuff we wouldn't normally do. For me, that means sports! But which one should I choose?

I leaned against a fence and watched two girls whacking a ball back and forth on a tennis court. Those girls were really working up a sweat (yuck). Maybe I wanted to try swimming instead.

"Great game, isn't it?" a voice behind me said.

I turned around. A boy was standing there, smiling at me. A very *cute* boy.

"Um, yeah." I stared into his blue, blue eyes.

"Do you play tennis?" he asked.

"A little," I lied. I didn't want to admit to this very athletic-looking guy that I wasn't good at sports. "How about you?"

He nodded. "I'm on the team here." He flashed me another gorgeous smile. "Tryouts are tomorrow, if you're interested."

Was I interested? With guys like him on the team? Definitely! Diary, who knows if I'll wind up liking tennis? But one thing's for sure. I could definitely wind up liking this guy!

Dear Diary,

"Look, there's the camp!" I said pointing through the trees. We were on a mission to steal back the founder's portrait from our rival camp. It was a tradition that had been going on for thirty years. And this year it was up to me and my friends to get it!

Right ahead of us was the mess hall, where the portrait hung over a big stone fireplace.

Blair clicked on her flashlight and shined it into the mess hall window. "Check it out!" she said.

Three kids were wrapped up in sleeping bags underneath the portrait. They were supposed to be guarding it. But they were all asleep!

This is going to be a piece of cake, I thought. But then—we got caught.

Win a **mary-kateandashley**
Spa Kit!

$100 value

Enter below to win everything you need to pamper yourself at your own private spa—all from the *mary-kateandashley* brand!

* Hair care products

* Hairdryer and curling iron

* Lip gloss, body glitter, eye shadow and more

* Fabulous hair accessories

TWO OF A KIND™
Spa Kit Sweepstakes

OFFICIAL RULES:

1. No purchase necessary.

2. To enter complete the official entry form or hand print your name, address, age, and phone number along with the words "TWO OF A KIND Spa Kit Sweepstakes" on a 3" x 5" card and mail to: TWO OF A KIND Spa Kit Sweepstakes, c/o HarperEntertainment, Attn: Children's Marketing Department, 10 East 53rd Street, New York, NY 10022. Entries must be received by July 31, 2003. Enter as often as you wish, but each entry must be mailed separately. One entry per envelope. Partially completed, illegible, or mechanically reproduced entries will not be accepted. Sponsors are not responsible for lost, late, mutilated, illegible, stolen, postage due, incomplete, or misdirected entries. All entries become the property of Dualstar Entertainment Group, LLC, and will not be returned.

3. Sweepstakes open to all legal residents of the United States, (excluding Colorado and Rhode Island), who are between the ages of five and fifteen on July 31, 2003, excluding employees and immediate family members of HarperCollins Publishers, Inc., ("HarperCollins"), Warner Bros.Television ("Warner"), Parachute Properties and Parachute Press, Inc., and their respective subsidiaries and affiliates, officers, directors, shareholders, employees, agents, attorneys, and other representatives (individually and collectively "Parachute"), Dualstar Entertainment Group, LLC, and its subsidiaries and affiliates, officers, directors, shareholders, employees, agents, attorneys, and other representatives (individually and collectively "Dualstar"), and their respective parent companies, affiliates, subsidiaries, advertising, promotion and fulfillment agencies, and the persons with whom each of the above are domiciled. Offer void where prohibited or restricted by law.

4. Odds of winning depend on the total number of entries received. Approximately 375,000 sweepstakes announcements published. All prizes will be awarded. Winners will be randomly drawn on or about August 15, 2003, by HarperCollins Publishers, whose decisions are final. Potential winners will be notified by mail and will be required to sign and return an affidavit of eligibility and release of liability within 14 days of notification. Prizes won by minors will be awarded to parent or legal guardian who must sign and return all required legal documents. By acceptance of their prize, winners consent to the use of their names, photographs, likeness, and personal information by HarperCollins, Parachute, Dualstar, and for publicity purposes without further compensation except where prohibited.

5. Five (5) **Grand Prize Winners** win a *mary-kateandashley* Spa Kit, which consists of $100.00 worth of *mary-kateandashley* brand beauty products to include: haircare products, hair appliances, cosmetics, and hair accessories. Approximate retail value of each prize is $100.00.

6. Only one prize will be awarded per individual, family, or household. Prizes are non-transferable and cannot be sold or redeemed for cash. No cash substitute is available. Any federal, state, or local taxes are the responsibility of the winner. Sponsor may substitute prize of equal or greater value, if necessary, due to availability.

7. Additional terms: By participating, entrants agree a) to the official rules and decisions of the judges, which will be final in all respects; and to waive any claim to ambiguity of the official rules and b) to release, discharge, and hold harmless HarperCollins, Warner, Parachute, Dualstar, and their affiliates, subsidiaries, and advertising and promotion agencies from and against any and all liability or damages associated with acceptance, use, or misuse of any prize received in this Sweepstakes.

8. Any dispute arising from this Sweepstakes will be determined according to the laws of the State of New York, without reference to its conflict of law principles, and the entrants consent to the personal jurisdiction of the State and Federal courts located in New York County and agree that such courts have exclusive jurisdiction over all such disputes.

9. To obtain the name of the winners, please send your request and a self-addressed stamped envelope (residents of Vermont may omit return postage) to TWO OF A KIND Spa Kit Sweepstakes Winners, c/o HarperEntertainment, 10 East 53rd Street, New York, NY 10022 by September 1, 2003. Sweepstakes Sponsor: HarperCollins Publishers, Inc.

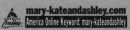

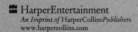

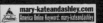